Dedicated to you. May you always find a reason to smile.

The Arcade Incident

A Retro Horrors: The Lost Decade

Book meant to be read in no particular order.

Written by B. Humphrey

The Arrival of Neon Abyss

Tommy Mitchell gripped his BMX handlebars, his fingers sticky from the cherry slushie he'd gulped down too fast. The hot August sun baked the blacktop of Sunset Hills Mall's parking lot, filling the air with the sour tang of spilled soda, hot tar, and cheap perfume. His Walkman bounced against his hip, the headphones crooked around his neck blasting Duran Duran's *Notorious*.

"Dude, you're late," Jake "Jinx" Miller groaned, flicking his mop of brown hair out of his eyes. He kicked his skateboard up into his hand, frustration thick in his voice. "We were supposed to meet *before* the arcade opened. I've got high scores to crush."

"Relax, Jinx," Tommy grinned, rolling his bike to a halt. "Pixel Palace ain't going anywhere. It's like, permanent."

Rae Dawson rolled her eyes from beneath her oversized aviators, a thick black ponytail falling over one shoulder. "Permanent like your math grade, Mitchell? C'mon, let's get inside before Jinx loses his mind."

The mall doors hissed open, and a wave of cool, conditioned air hit them like a blessing. The smell inside the mall was something else: cinnamon pretzels from Auntie Anne's, hot cheese from Galaxy Pizza, and the faintest whiff of stale popcorn from the movie theater two wings down.

"Okay, bet you guys five bucks I hit the top score on *Pac-Man* today," Tony Lopez said, adjusting the strap of his dad's old VHS camcorder on his shoulder. The thing was clunky and awkward, but he refused to leave it behind. "And if I do, Rae has to admit *Back to the Future* is better than *Ghostbusters*."

Rae shot him a withering glance. "Dream on, Spielberg. You couldn't beat *Pac-Man* if your joystick had cheat codes." Jinx snickered, giving Tony a playful nudge as the group strode toward their haven: *The Pixel Palace*.

The neon sign over the arcade flickered, buzzing faintly. Inside, the world seemed to come alive with the steady hum of machines, the clatter of quarters dropping into coin slots, and the bleeps and bloops of endless 8-bit games. Kids huddled around cabinets like disciples at church, each lost in pursuit of digital immortality.

Jinx cracked his knuckles and zeroed in on *Galaga*. Rae veered toward *Centipede*, her fingers itching for the familiar glide of the trackball. Tommy stood still for a moment, taking it all in—the strobing lights, the glowing screens, the faint, acrid scent of burnt plastic.

And then, like a big bright neon distraction he saw it. In the back corner, where no cabinet had been before, stood a game unlike any Tommy had ever seen. The machine's screen glitched and swirled with colors too vibrant to belong to the real world—neon greens bleeding into pinks, like the Northern Lights trapped inside a CRT monitor. Above the screen, the title blinked in jagged letters: **NEON ABYSS**.

"Whoa," Tommy whispered, stepping closer.

The cabinet hummed as if it were alive. The joystick twitched slightly, almost imperceptibly. It was calling to him—like the siren song of forbidden treasure. He didn't know how, but he could feel it: This game was different. "Guys, check this out," he called over his shoulder. Jinx skated over, dragging his board behind him. "What the—? I don't remember this game being here yesterday."

"No one does," added Rae, narrowing her eyes. "It's not even on the high-score list." Tommy pressed his face closer to the glass. The screen blinked, pixels rearranging like pieces of a puzzle—random patterns coalescing into strange shapes, twisted cities, and eyes staring back. He shivered, the hairs on the back of his neck standing on end.

"Okay, this thing is *creepy*," Tony said, lifting his camcorder. The red recording light flicked on. "Neon Abyss... looks like a bad dream."

"Or an *awesome* one," Jinx grinned, slamming a quarter into the slot. "Watch this, suckers. High score, here I come."

The game booted with a strange, warped jingle—a chime that started high but ended in a low, vibrating hum that Tommy swore he could feel in his bones. Jinx grabbed the joystick, and the screen flashed to life.

Level One.

A low-resolution cityscape scrolled across the screen, populated with flickering shadows and static figures. Jinx moved his avatar—a neon-blue figure with a jagged, glitching outline—through the streets. Strange creatures—half-animal, half-machine—leapt from the alleys, and the game demanded split-second reactions.

"Dude, this is unreal!" Jinx whooped, twisting the joystick. His face was lit by the glowing screen, his eyes wide and unblinking. "I've never seen graphics this good." The others crowded around him, captivated by the hypnotic swirl of colors and motion. The sound effects were unlike anything from other games—whispers layered over synth tones, like fragments of a distant conversation just out of reach.

"Do you hear that?" Rae whispered. Tommy nodded. The game wasn't just making sounds—it was speaking. Or at least, it felt like it was. Jinx leaned further into the machine, his hands glued to the joystick, eyes flickering with every pixel shift. As the level progressed, the creatures on screen grew more unsettling—faces that seemed too human, hands reaching out through the static.

"Almost got it... almost..." Jinx muttered, his voice distant, as if he were slipping into the game itself. The glow from the screen deepened, casting long shadows across his face. And then—without warning—the screen glitched violently, flashing bright white. Jinx's hands jerked away from the controls. The machine powered down with a low hum, as if exhaling. For a moment, the air felt thicker, heavy with static.

"What the hell?" Jinx muttered, rubbing his eyes. He swore under his breath and gave the cabinet a frustrated slap. "That... was weird," Tommy said, his heart racing. He didn't know why, but something about the game felt *wrong*. The way it ended, the way it pulled at Jinx—like it had almost swallowed him whole. Tony adjusted his camcorder. "Got all of that on tape. Something tells me this thing isn't exactly... normal."

"Normal is overrated," Jinx scoffed, though there was a nervous edge to his voice. "I'm coming back tomorrow. I'm gonna crush this thing." Rae crossed her arms. "I don't know, guys. This game... it's giving me the creeps."

"Creeps or not, I need that high score," Jinx said, slapping Tony on the back. "You can film my victory."

Tommy couldn't shake the feeling that the game had been watching them—that it was waiting for them to come back.

As they left the arcade, a pair of eyes followed their retreat—the glowing red security monitor perched above the door. And somewhere in the shadows of the mall, Phil the security guard adjusted his belt, a knowing smile playing across his lips.

The kids pedaled home that night beneath a sky painted with streaks of orange and pink, BMX tires humming against the pavement. Tommy kept glancing back toward the mall, unable to shake the strange weight sitting in his chest. *Neon Abyss* wasn't just a game—it was something else. Something dangerous.

The synth-heavy tunes of his Walkman couldn't drown out the whisper that had lodged itself in his mind: *Come back.* And Tommy knew, even as the sun dipped below the horizon, that they would.

They always did.

Chapter Two: Token Trouble

Tommy Mitchell tapped his Converse sneakers against the sticky linoleum floor of **Galaxy Pizza**, chewing absentmindedly on a piece of gum that had lost its flavor twenty minutes ago. The air inside the food court was thick with grease and sugar, mixing the smell of cheesy pizza with caramel popcorn and fresh soda fizz. Around him, the mall buzzed with Saturday energy—teenagers laughing too loud, kids begging for quarters, and moms dragging toddlers in strollers past the glowing storefronts of Suncoast Video and Spencer's.

"Where is he?" Tommy muttered, spinning a greasy pepperoni slice in its cardboard tray. "Jinx should've been here by now."

"Bet he's still trying to beat that game." **Rae Dawson** leaned back in her plastic chair, the oversized aviators perched on her head catching the fluorescent lights above. She looked bored, but Tommy could tell she was worried. Rae didn't do "worried" out loud—it showed up in little things, like her tapping nails against the table or chewing the inside of her cheek.

"Dude's obsessed." **Tony Lopez**, clutching his dad's heavy camcorder, kicked his legs up on the table like he owned the place. The weight of the camera made him sit slightly lopsided. "Neon Abyss is all he talked about on the way home yesterday. Said he felt like he was *this close* to cracking the final level."

"Yeah, well, maybe *this close* got him sucked into the Matrix," Rae said, folding her arms. "It's not normal to skip pizza day. Jinx lives for pizza day."

Tommy glanced at the arcade entrance across the food court. The neon sign for **The Pixel Palace** blinked erratically, casting strange shadows along the mall tile. Normally, the sight would make his heart race with excitement, but today, it just made his stomach twist. "Something's weird," Tommy mumbled.

"You mean weird like *mysterious vanishing arcade cabinets* weird, or weird like *Jinx isn't answering his phone* weird?" Rae asked, though she already knew the answer. Tony fiddled with the camcorder's lens. "I say we go back to the arcade. Maybe he's just so deep into that game he forgot the time."

Tommy didn't buy it. Jinx was reckless, sure—but not *disappearing-on-pizza-day* reckless. "I bet Phil knows something." Tommy's voice was low, but the name made Rae groan. "Ugh, not Phil. That guy's a creep." "Exactly," Tommy said. "He creeps because he knows stuff." Tony adjusted his camcorder with a grin. "Let's go shake him down."

The arcade felt *different* as soon as they walked inside. The familiar clatter of machines and the cheerful bleeps of games sounded distant, muted. A strange hum filled the air—a buzz just low enough to crawl under Tommy's skin.

The kids wandered past the rows of glowing cabinets, their footsteps echoing in a place that was never supposed to be this quiet. Rae's gaze darted around, sharp and suspicious, while Tony kept his camcorder rolling. "No Jinx," Rae muttered. "You don't think..."

Tommy's eyes landed on the corner where **Neon Abyss** sat, glowing like a trap in the dark. The swirling colors on the screen twisted and shifted, making Tommy's stomach lurch, like standing too close to the edge of a cliff. "He was here." Tony zoomed the camera in on the cabinet. "The tokens are still warm."

"Not funny, Tony," Rae snapped, though her eyes stayed locked on the game. Tommy stepped closer to the cabinet. Something about it called to him again, the way it had the day before. He could almost hear the faint whisper of music from inside the screen, like a warped cassette tape playing backward.

He reached out—and the machine powered on without warning, the screen flashing to life with a burst of static. *Level One: Begin.* "Okay," Rae said, backing away. "That's enough creepy for one day. Let's go find Phil."

Phil was exactly where they expected to find him—leaning against the mall's service desk, his dark blue security uniform stained with coffee and his bald head gleaming under the overhead lights. His walkie-talkie crackled with static, but he ignored it, swirling the last dregs of a Mountain Dew around the bottom of a Styrofoam cup.

"Back again, huh?" Phil's voice was lazy and slow, like a man who'd seen too much and cared too little. "You kids really ought to stay outta trouble."

"We're looking for Jinx," Tommy said, planting himself in front of the old man. "He's not at the arcade. You seen him?" Phil gave them a look—one of those long, unreadable stares that made the back of Tommy's neck itch. "Maybe," Phil said finally. "Maybe not." Rae groaned, stepping forward. "Cut the creepy act, Phil. You know that we know you know stuff and junk."

"Careful, kid." Phil's grin was slow and toothy, like a wolf pretending not to be hungry. "You poke around too much, you might not like what you find."

"Listen," Tommy said, trying to keep his cool. "Jinx has been missing since he played that weird new game, and we know something's up with it. So how about you stop being a weirdo and tell us what you know?" Phil chuckled—a deep, gravelly sound that made Tommy want to punch him.

"All I'll say is, some games... they ain't meant to be beaten." He tossed his empty cup into the trash and leaned in close, the scent of stale soda and cheap cologne wafting off him. "You kids ever hear of a place called the Abyss?"

Tony's eyes widened behind the camcorder, and Rae gave Tommy a nervous glance. Phil smirked. "Yeah. Thought not." Without another word, he turned and sauntered off, whistling a tuneless song that echoed in the empty hall.

Back in the arcade, the kids huddled around **Neon Abyss**, the machine's glow flickering against their anxious faces. Tommy pulled a crumpled five-dollar bill from his pocket and fed it into the token machine. The tokens clattered into the metal tray with a satisfying *clink-clink-clink*. "I'm going in," Tommy said, his jaw set. Rae grabbed his arm. "Wait—what do you think you're doing?"

"We need to know what happened to Jinx." Tommy's eyes were hard. "And if this game is connected, I have to play it." Tony shrugged, hoisting the camcorder onto his shoulder. "Well, if you get sucked into the Twilight Zone, at least I'll have it all on tape." Tommy gave Rae a small grin. "Thanks for the vote of confidence."

With a deep breath, he dropped a token into the slot. The machine whirred to life, the screen flashing in rapid bursts of neon light. His fingers gripped the joystick as the first level began.

The familiar cityscape scrolled across the screen, but this time it felt... off. The shadows seemed longer, the streets more twisted. And in the distance, he could see something watching him from the static—a pair of glowing red eyes that blinked slowly, like a predator waiting for the right moment to pounce.

"Okay, Tommy," he whispered to himself. "Let's do this." The game's music shifted into a strange, low hum—a sound that rattled in his chest. His avatar moved through the streets, dodging strange creatures that flickered in and out of existence like ghosts trapped between worlds.

Then the screen glitched. For a moment, everything froze. The joystick locked in place, and the shadows on the screen stretched toward him, clawing their way out of the machine.

"Tommy?" Rae's voice sounded far away, like she was speaking through a tunnel. The screen flashed again, and suddenly Tommy wasn't in the arcade anymore. He was somewhere else. Somewhere dark.

And something was waiting for him.

Chapter 3: Into the Glitch

The world around Tommy shifted like a bad TV signal—flickering, distorting, and warping in and out of focus. His hands, still gripping the joystick, felt distant, as if they didn't belong to him. The colors on the screen twisted into impossible shapes: neon tendrils curling, streets coiling and folding into themselves like a city inside a dream—or a nightmare. And then, with a final snap, the arcade disappeared entirely.

Tommy blinked. He was no longer standing in front of **Neon Abyss**. Instead, he stood in the middle of a cold, dark street. Overhead, the sky shimmered with strange static clouds, and a dim, purple glow bathed the cityscape in eerie light. The buildings were warped and stretched at impossible angles, like reflections seen through a funhouse mirror. His heart raced as he realized: **He was inside the game.**

The streets stretched endlessly in both directions, flickering with faint neon signs in languages he couldn't read. In the distance, the sound of glitching whispers—broken fragments of words and strange electronic noises—drifted through the heavy air.

"Hello?" Tommy's voice cracked, swallowed up by the endless emptiness. "Jinx? You out here?" No response—just the low hum of the game's soundtrack, vibrating in his bones like the bass line of a cassette tape turned up too loud. He started walking, the soles of his shoes slapping against the cracked, glowing pavement.

Shapes flickered in the corners of Tommy's vision, shifting like shadows that refused to stay still. As he moved deeper into the glitchy city, something caught his eye—a blue figure standing at the end of the street, illuminated by a flickering streetlight.

"Jinx?" Tommy called, hope rising in his chest. He sprinted toward the figure, his heart pounding against his ribs. The closer he got, the more wrong it seemed. The figure wore Jinx's clothes—his favorite *Defender* t-shirt and shredded jeans—but the face wasn't quite right. It twitched and flickered, like pixels that hadn't loaded properly.

Tommy stopped in his tracks, his breath catching in his throat. "Tommy..." The voice was Jinx's—distorted and slow, like a VHS tape left out in the sun too long. The figure tilted its head, a jerky, unnatural motion. "You shouldn't be here..."

"Jinx, what happened to you?" Tommy whispered.

The figure glitched, stuttering forward with a series of static pops. "The game... It doesn't let you leave." Meanwhile, in **The Pixel Palace**, Rae paced back and forth in front of the **Neon Abyss** machine, her arms crossed tightly over her chest. "This is bad. This is *really* bad." Tony adjusted his camcorder, the lens focused on the flickering screen. "We should pull him out," he suggested, though he had no idea how. "He's been in there too long."

"How?" Rae snapped. "It's not like there's an eject button!" Tony leaned closer to the machine. The screen showed Tommy's avatar wandering through the glitchy city, his pixelated form small and vulnerable against the twisted landscape. "I don't think this is just a game," Tony muttered. "This is... something else."

"No kidding." Rae smacked the side of the cabinet in frustration. "Phil knows something about this—something he's not telling us." Tony gave her a grim look. "Then we'd better get answers, fast."

Inside the game, Tommy stumbled backward as the glitched version of Jinx flickered and dissolved into static. He was alone again—except for the whispers. They grew louder, circling him like a swarm of invisible insects.

He ran, feet pounding against the glowing pavement, heart slamming in his chest. The city shifted around him, streets curling into labyrinths, buildings warping like they were made of liquid glass. There was no way out—only deeper into the game.

And then, just as the shadows began to close in, Tommy spotted **a glowing doorway** at the end of a narrow alley, pulsing with bright neon light. Without thinking, he sprinted toward it, every instinct screaming that this was his only chance.

The neon doorway shimmered, its edges flickering with bursts of static. Tommy reached out, and the door swallowed him whole in a flash of blinding light.

He tumbled through the air, weightless, and landed hard on a glowing platform in what looked like the inside of a giant machine—gears turning slowly, cables snaking across the walls like veins.

"Level Two," a robotic voice whispered from nowhere and everywhere at once. "Welcome to the Abyss." Tommy groaned, rubbing his head. This was worse than any video game he'd ever played. The stakes weren't just high—they were real. If he didn't beat the game, he wasn't getting out.

Back in the real world, Rae was already halfway out of the arcade, dragging Tony behind her. "Come on—we need to find Phil," she said, her voice sharp with urgency. "If anyone knows how to get Tommy out, it's him." Tony stumbled along, still clutching his camcorder. "And what if he doesn't tell us?" Rae's jaw tightened. "Then we *make* him tell us."

They found Phil lurking by the service desk again, looking far too smug for Rae's liking. She marched right up to him and jabbed a finger into his chest. "What's going on with that game, Phil? And how do we get our friend out of it?"

Phil chuckled, the sound low and greasy. "Told ya, some games ain't meant to be beaten." Tony raised his camcorder, the red-light blinking. "If you don't start talking, Phil, you're gonna be famous. Mall security guard implicated in creepy game scandal—front-page news."

Phil's grin faded. "Alright, alright." He leaned closer, dropping his voice to a conspiratorial whisper. "Neon Abyss isn't just a game—it's a trap. Built to pull in the curious, the brave, the reckless. And once you're inside..."

"You can't leave," Rae finished, her heart sinking. Phil nodded, his eyes dark with something close to regret. "Your only shot is to beat it. But no one ever has."

Inside the game, Tommy was running again—this time through a maze of shifting gears and glitching walls. The whispers grew louder, more desperate, as shadowy figures emerged from the static, reaching for him with pixelated hands.

He ducked and weaved, heart pounding, as the platform beneath his feet began to crumble. The exit was just ahead—another glowing door, pulsing with the promise of escape. With one final burst of speed, Tommy leapt through the door, the shadows snapping at his heels. Tommy landed in a dimly lit corridor, the air thick with static. The walls pulsed with strange symbols—runes that flickered like dying neon signs.

He knew what this meant. **Level Three.** And somewhere, deep within the game, **Jinx was waiting for him.** But Tommy wasn't leaving without him.

Not this time.

Chapter 4: Finding the Loop

The hum of the **Pixel Palace's** neon lights buzzed in the back of Tommy's mind, even though he was miles away—lost inside the swirling, corrupted world of **Neon Abyss.** Every breath felt sharp, metallic, like breathing in static electricity, and the floor beneath his feet shifted with every step, as if the game were alive and rearranging itself beneath him.

Somewhere in this digital nightmare, **Jinx** was out there, trapped—and Tommy knew, deep in his gut, that getting out wouldn't be easy.

The corridor stretched out endlessly in both directions, the walls flashing symbols that flickered like old television static. Tommy's pulse pounded in his ears. This place wasn't just a game—it felt deliberate, like every twist and dead-end was *designed* to get inside his head. He ran his hand along the cold wall, and it responded with a strange hiss, like it knew he was there. "Okay, Jinx... where the hell are you?"

A low noise echoed from somewhere deep in the maze—an unsettling blend of robotic beeps and *something else.* Something alive. Tommy kept moving, but the walls shifted with him, doors slamming shut behind him while new ones appeared ahead. It was a **loop**, repeating over and over. The game wasn't just making him play—it was **messing with his mind.**

A flickering neon sign overhead pulsed with jagged letters: *FEED YOUR FEAR.* Tommy swallowed hard, forcing down the rising panic. The walls rippled again, and out of the corner of his eye, he saw a figure—just for a second. A flash of blue. **Jinx.**

"Jinx!" Tommy called out, sprinting toward the shadow. But just as he reached the end of the corridor, the walls blinked again—Jinx disappeared into the static, and Tommy found himself right back where he'd started, staring at the same twisted symbols. He was **caught in a loop.**

Meanwhile, **Rae** and **Tony** were back at **Sunset Hills Mall**, squeezing every last drop of info they could get outta Phil. "The game... it wasn't supposed to be here. It's part of something... older. **A glitch in the system**—not just the arcade, but the whole mall. The game feeds on people—pulls them in, traps them in loops, and never lets go."

"Then how do we beat it?" Rae demanded, her fists clenched. "You don't beat it," Phil said with a grim chuckle. "You survive it—*if* you're lucky." Rae's heart sank. They were running out of time. Tommy wasn't just playing a game—he was trapped inside something alive, something hungry. And if they didn't get him out soon, he'd be lost forever.

Inside **Neon Abyss**, Tommy pressed on, fighting the urge to give up as the walls of the maze folded in on themselves again and again. He could feel the game pressing down on him, wearing him out—like it wanted him to fail. But then he remembered something Jinx always said whenever they were stuck in **The Legend of Zelda**: *"When a game messes with you, you mess right back."*

Tommy took a deep breath, closed his eyes, and stopped running. The walls shuddered around him, as if confused. He stepped forward, calmly now, ignoring the twisted doorways and flickering symbols.

Instead of running from the loop, he walked **into it**—trusting that the only way out was through. The walls groaned and bent as if the game were trying to resist him, but Tommy kept going, step by deliberate step.

And just like that, the loop shattered. The corridor snapped back into place, revealing a door at the end—a neon-framed portal glowing bright with jagged blues and greens. "Gotcha," Tommy whispered, a grin spreading across his face. He sprinted toward the door and threw himself through it—plunging headfirst into the next level.

When Tommy landed, he found himself inside **the mall**—but not the one he knew. This version of Sunset Hills Mall was twisted beyond recognition. The food court was empty, the escalators led to nowhere, and the storefronts flickered in and out of existence.

Neon signs glowed with strange, shifting words: *SALE!* became *TRAPPED!* in the blink of an eye. **Galaxy Pizza** looked warped, the chairs melting into puddles of static, and the mannequins in the windows of Spencer's twisted their heads to follow Tommy as he walked past.

"Hello?" Tommy called out, his voice bouncing off the empty walls. Rounding a corner, he thought he saw a flash of blue up ahead. **Jinx.** "Jinx!" Tommy sprinted across the warped food court, weaving past glitching furniture and neon puddles. This time, when he reached his friend, the figure didn't dissolve into static.

Jinx turned slowly, his face pale and drawn, his eyes flickering with the same glitchy static as the walls. "Tommy..." he whispered, his voice broken and hollow. "It's too late. You shouldn't have come."

"Don't say that, man," Tommy said, grabbing Jinx's shoulder. "I'm getting you out of here. Both of us." Jinx gave a sad smile. "You can't. The game... it doesn't let anyone leave." Back in the real world, Rae and Tony stared Phil down, frustration boiling over. "What aren't you telling us, Phil?" Rae demanded. "How do we end this?"

Phil hesitated for a long moment, then leaned in close, his voice barely above a whisper. "I told you, you don't beat the game, you survive it—**by finishing it.** But you won't like what's waiting at the end." Rae narrowed her eyes. "What's waiting at the end?" Phil smiled, but it wasn't a kind smile. "Not everyone who plays gets to leave."

Inside the game, Tommy felt the walls close in again. He could sense the game's impatience—it wanted to trap him, to break him, but Tommy wouldn't let it. "Come on, Jinx," Tommy said, pulling his friend along. "We're beating this thing. Together." The neon lights around them flickered violently, as if the game were fighting back. But Tommy didn't care. He had one shot, and he wasn't letting it slip away.

He saw the next doorway—a jagged tear in reality, glowing with fierce green light—and sprinted toward it with Jinx at his side. The game roared, the walls crumbling and folding in on themselves in a final, desperate attempt to trap them. But Tommy was faster. He grabbed Jinx's hand, and together, they **jumped through the portal**—just as the world of **Neon Abyss** collapsed behind them.

Tommy hit the ground hard, gasping for breath. He blinked against the harsh glow of arcade lights—and realized he was back. He lay sprawled on the linoleum floor of **The Pixel Palace**, Jinx beside him, both of them panting and disoriented.

The **Neon Abyss** machine stood silent, its screen dark and lifeless. The game was over. For now. But as Tommy sat up, he noticed something chilling: **the glow of the arcade cabinet**—just barely visible, a faint flicker of neon green, like a machine waiting... for the next player.

Chapter 5: VHS Clues and Secret Levels

The familiar hum of the **Pixel Palace** arcade filled Tommy's ears as he lay sprawled on the linoleum floor, catching his breath. His chest rose and fell like he'd just finished a race—except this race had been through a nightmare stitched together from pixels and static. Beside him, **Jinx** groaned, clutching his head as if waking from a bad dream. The flickering glow of **Neon Abyss** had dimmed, but Tommy swore he could feel the game still watching, lurking, waiting for someone foolish enough to try it again. Tony's camcorder lens zoomed in, catching every ragged breath and jittery movement. "Dude, that was... intense."

"Intense? It was like *getting swallowed alive!*" Jinx croaked, wiping sweat from his brow. "What the hell just happened in there?" Rae knelt beside them, glaring at the now-silent cabinet. "You tell us. What's inside that thing?"

Tommy shook his head, struggling to piece together the fragmented memories of the game's warped city streets, looping corridors, and eerie neon signs. "It wasn't just a game... it was like being trapped inside... I don't know, *a maze built out of fear.*"

Jinx looked rattled, his usual cocky grin replaced with something brittle. "It didn't feel like a game. It felt... alive." Later that night, the gang regrouped in **Tony's basement**, a haven cluttered with comic books, VHS tapes, and old pizza boxes. The faint glow of a tube TV cast flickering shadows across the walls. Tony's camcorder sat hooked up to the TV, ready to play back the footage from the arcade. "Alright," Tony said, settling onto the carpet and hitting play. "Let's see what we've got."

The footage began with shaky shots of **Neon Abyss**, the warped colors on the screen shimmering like an oil slick under a flickering streetlight. At first, everything looked ordinary—just kids crowded around an arcade machine. But then the footage glitched, colors twisting into strange patterns. The familiar hum of the arcade grew distorted, the sounds slowing into a low, ominous tone.

Suddenly, the screen on the camcorder **froze**—the game cabinet's colors spiraling outward like a hypnotic vortex. Tommy's image on the screen jerked toward the machine, eyes wide with fear as if something unseen had grabbed him, like the scene where Jaws tugs at a guy one time before swallowing him whole. And then, just as quickly, the image blinked to static. "What the hell was that?" Rae muttered, leaning closer to the TV. Tony rewound the footage. "There—see? It's like the game... *pulled you in.* That's not normal."

"No kidding," Jinx grumbled, shivering at the memory. "And it didn't just pull us in—it messed with our heads. I kept seeing things—stuff from my past. Bad memories." - "It's like the game knows what you're afraid of," Tommy whispered. "And it uses that against you." The room fell silent, the only sound the hum of the TV.

Tony paused the footage on a glitchy frame—the moment just before the cabinet had sucked Tommy in. In the middle of the distorted pixels, something flickered—barely visible, but there. A symbol. "Wait... what is that?" Rae asked, leaning closer to the screen.

Tony zoomed in. The symbol resembled **an eye, encircled by jagged lines**, like a cross between a circuit diagram and ancient runes. It flickered for only a fraction of a second, but its presence felt deliberate.

"Ever see anything like that?" Tommy asked. "Nope." Tony shook his head. "Not in any game I've played."

"That's because it's not just a game," Rae said grimly. "It's... something else." Jinx frowned. "What kind of arcade game comes with ancient symbols?"

"The cursed kind," Tony muttered. Rae gave him a deadpan look. "Thanks, Captain Obvious." Tommy's thoughts drifted back to **Danny Fletcher**, the quiet kid who had gone missing just a few days ago. Everyone said he had been playing in **The Pixel Palace** before he vanished. At the time, no one had connected his disappearance with the arrival of **Neon Abyss**. Now, it felt obvious.

"What if Danny's still in there?" Tommy said quietly. "Like... trapped inside the game, just like we were." Rae looked skeptical but worried. "If he is, how do we get him out?" Tony rewound the footage again, this time frame by frame. "There's gotta be a way. Games have secrets, right? Hidden levels, cheat codes, all that stuff."

Jinx perked up. "Yeah—like those secret levels in *Donkey Kong* or the kill screen in *Pac-Man*! There's gotta be some way to unlock whatever this game is hiding." Tony nodded. "Exactly. But we need to figure out what triggers it."

"We go back," Tommy said suddenly, his voice resolute. The others stared at him like he'd just suggested they ride their BMX bikes off a cliff. "Back?" Jinx scoffed. "Are you crazy? We barely made it out alive the first time!"

"We have to," Tommy insisted. "If Danny's in there, we can't just leave him. And… if this game's feeding off fear, we can't let it win." Rae chewed her lip, thinking. "Alright. But if we're doing this, we need to be smart about it. No more just charging in."

Tony grinned, holding up his camcorder. "And I'm bringing this baby with me. If we're going down, we're going down *documented.*" Jinx groaned. "Great. We'll be famous… if we survive."

Before heading back to the arcade, they decided to pay **Phil** another visit. The old security guard was still at his usual post, slouched behind the service desk looking greasy with his Styrofoam cup of soda. Phil smirked as they approached. "Figured you kids would be back. Gluttons for punishment, huh?"

"Save the creepy act," Rae said, crossing her arms. "We know the game's a trap. We just need to know how to break it." Phil's smile faded. "You don't break it, kid. You outsmart it."

"And how do we do that?" Tommy asked. Phil leaned closer, lowering his voice. "The game runs on **loops**—repeating the same patterns over and over. If you want to beat it, you gotta find the **secret level** hidden in the loop. But here's the catch: you don't find the secret level… it finds you."

"Great," Jinx muttered. "So we're basically walking into a death trap." Phil shrugged. "Ain't life a game?" Later that night, back in Tony's basement, the group gathered their gear: flashlights, snacks, Tony's camcorder, and a handful of quarters. Rae scribbled down notes from the footage, looking for patterns in the game's glitches.

Tommy felt the weight of what they were about to do pressing down on him, but he didn't back down. Danny Fletcher was out there. And the game wasn't going to win. "We do this together," he said, looking at his friends. "No bailing halfway through." Jinx gave him a weak smile. "Yeah, yeah. Ride or die, right?"

"Ride or die," Rae echoed, giving Jinx a playful shove.

Tony hit record on his camcorder, the red light blinking like a heartbeat. "Alright, guys. Let's get some answers."

They piled onto their BMX bikes and sped off toward the mall under the flickering glow of streetlights. The cool night air smelled like ozone and adventure, filling their lungs with a strange mix of fear and excitement. The arcade was waiting.

And this time, they were ready for it.

Chapter 6: Into the Neon Abyss

The air in **Sunset Hills Mall** felt different at night. The hum of fluorescent lights buzzed louder, and the stores—silent and dark—seemed to lurk in the shadows, waiting for something. The gang coasted into the parking lot on their BMX bikes, the cool night air tingling against their skin. The only sound was the whir of their wheels and the faint rattling of Tony's camcorder against his chest. Rae skidded to a stop at the side entrance. "Alright, we're here. Everyone got what they need?" Tony patted his camcorder like it was a lucky charm. "Got it."

"Flashlights?" Tommy asked, rummaging through his backpack. "Check." Rae flicked hers on, casting a thin beam of light through the cracked glass of the mall's side door. Jinx rolled his eyes. "You sure we need flashlights? We're breaking into a **mall**—not spelunking through a haunted cave."

"This *is* spelunking, dumbass," Rae shot back. "The kind where the cave tries to eat you." Jinx chuckled nervously, but the grin didn't reach his eyes. They all knew what was waiting for them inside—and it wasn't just another game.

The entrance groaned as Rae jimmied it open with a flathead screwdriver, the metal protesting like it hadn't moved in years. A gust of stale, air-conditioned air hit them as the door gave way, ushering them into the darkened mall.

The familiar layout of **Sunset Hills Mall** felt wrong under the cover of night. The food court tables were pushed to strange angles, mannequins loomed in store windows like silent watchers, and the glowing EXIT signs flickered, casting eerie green light on the tiled floor.

"It's way creepier when it's closed," Tony whispered, his voice almost swallowed by the empty space. "No kidding," Tommy said, gripping the strap of his backpack a little tighter. "Let's get to the arcade before something... changes." The group moved quickly through the empty corridors, their sneakers squeaking against the linoleum.

"There it is," Rae whispered as the glowing sign of **The Pixel Palace** flickered into view ahead. They stepped through the threshold, and the hum of the arcade enveloped them. The machines stood silent, their screens dark and lifeless—except for one.

Neon Abyss.

The cabinet buzzed faintly, its glitching screen swirling with bright neon colors that seemed to pulse like a heartbeat. Tommy felt a familiar tug in his gut—the game was calling him again. "Okay," Rae said, pulling out a notebook and flipping to the sketches she had made of the symbols from the VHS footage. "If we're right, the trick is finding that **hidden level** inside the loop." Jinx gave a mock salute. "No pressure, right?"

Tommy stepped forward and fed a coin into the slot. The machine came to life with a low hum, the screen flashing wildly before stabilizing into a familiar neon cityscape. The robotic voice echoed from the machine: **Level One: Begin.** "Here we go," Tommy muttered, gripping the joystick.

This time, the streets of the game-world felt more sinister, more alive—like they knew he had returned. The shadows stretched longer, the static buzzed louder, and the neon signs flickered with strange new messages: **TURN BACK** and **YOU DON'T BELONG HERE.**

Tony adjusted the camcorder, capturing everything. "Remember, the loop resets when you follow it. You need to do something different—break the pattern." Tommy nodded. His hands moved smoothly over the controls, guiding his avatar through the maze-like streets, dodging the half-human, half-digital creatures lurking in the shadows.

As Tommy moved deeper into the game, the screen flickered violently, and a new message scrolled across the top: **SECRET LEVEL UNLOCKED.** Rae leaned closer. "You found it." The neon city flickered, twisting itself into something else entirely. The walls folded, and Tommy's avatar tumbled through the floor, landing inside **a warped version of the mall.**

The new level was a perfect copy of **Sunset Hills Mall**—but corrupted. Escalators spiraled upward endlessly, food court tables glitched in and out of existence, and the storefronts displayed unsettling messages: **LOST FOREVER** and **ALL WHO ENTER ARE TRAPPED.**

"It's... us," Tommy whispered. "The game knows where we are." A chill ran down his spine as he guided the avatar through the glitching hallways. In the distance, he spotted a figure—a flickering blue outline. **Danny Fletcher.** "There!" Tommy shouted, pointing at the screen. "It's Danny!"

Tommy moved the joystick with precision, guiding his avatar closer to Danny's flickering figure. But just as he reached him, the screen glitched again—Danny's form dissolved into static, replaced by a new figure: **Jinx's avatar.**

"What the hell?" Jinx whispered, stepping closer to the screen. Suddenly, the game roared to life, and the **Neon Abyss** cabinet began to shake violently, sparks flying from the edges. The screen flashed:

FINAL LEVEL: COMPLETE THE CIRCLE.

The arcade around them seemed to shimmer, and for a split second, the group could see **two versions of the mall** overlapping—one real, one digital. The walls flickered, the floor trembled, and the air hummed with static. "We're inside the game," Rae whispered, her voice trembling. "It's pulling us in." - "Get ready," Tommy said, his heart hammering in his chest. "We have to jump."

"Jump?" Jinx cried. "Into what?!"

"Into the loop." Tommy's eyes locked on the screen as the glitching door to the final level flickered in and out of view. "We finish the circle. That's how we beat it." Before anyone could protest, Tommy grabbed the joystick and plunged his avatar through the glowing doorway—just as the cabinet erupted with a final burst of neon light.

In an instant, the world around them blinked—and they were no longer standing in the arcade. They were **inside the game.** The warped version of Sunset Hills Mall loomed all around them, its walls buzzing with static, its corridors stretching endlessly in every direction. But now they weren't just avatars. They were *themselves*, trapped in the game's twisted reality.

The glowing message scrolled across the walls: **ONLY ONE CAN LEAVE.** "Oh, this just keeps getting better," Jinx muttered, his voice shaky. Tommy clenched his fists. "We're not playing by its rules. We're breaking the loop—together."

The walls flickered violently, and a shadowy figure emerged from the static—**Danny Fletcher**, his eyes glowing with eerie blue light. He pointed toward the nearest exit, his voice a hollow whisper:

"Finish the game... or it finishes you." The group ran, weaving through glitching storefronts and endless hallways, the shadows chasing them with every step. The neon signs overhead flashed wildly, taunting them with words like **NO ESCAPE** and **YOU'RE TOO LATE.**

But Tommy knew better now. The game thrived on fear—fed off it. If they wanted to win, they had to face it head-on. With a deep breath, Tommy led the group through the final portal, their bodies humming with static as the world folded around them. The screen blinked one last time: **GAME OVER.** And then—just like that—they were back.

The gang collapsed on the linoleum floor of the **Pixel Palace**, gasping for breath. The **Neon Abyss** machine sat silent and dark, its screen shattered, sparks flickering at the edges.

Jinx let out a shaky laugh. "We did it... we actually did it." Rae sat up, still catching her breath. "Yeah. But something tells me this isn't over." Tommy glanced at the machine, unease prickling at the back of his mind. He could feel it—the faintest hum of static, like a song that hadn't quite ended.

The game was over. But **the Abyss** was still waiting.

Chapter 7: The Mall Beneath

The silence of **The Pixel Palace** was unsettling. The gang sat in a loose circle on the arcade's sticky linoleum floor, their breath still uneven, nerves raw. The shattered screen of **Neon Abyss** flickered one last time, then blinked off, leaving only a thin trail of smoke curling from the broken monitor.

But Tommy knew, deep down in his gut, that the game wasn't really gone. It had only retreated—waiting. Jinx rubbed his face and muttered, "Well, that was *something*. Can we all agree to never touch another arcade machine ever again?"

Rae shot him a withering look. "You think it's that simple? You saw the same thing I did—this isn't just a broken game. There's more to it." She glanced toward the far wall, where the outline of a door was barely visible through the shadows. Tommy followed her gaze. "What if... the game was just a **doorway**?" His voice was quiet, but it carried weight. "And we're not done yet."

Tony clicked off his camcorder and slung it over his shoulder. "I hate when you get that look, dude. Every time you do, it means trouble." Rae stood up and dusted off her jeans. "C'mon. If that door leads somewhere, we need to know where it goes."

The gang approached the dark corner of the arcade where the **Neon Abyss** cabinet had stood. Now that the game was destroyed, the wall behind it shimmered strangely, like static clinging to the air. "Okay, seriously," Jinx said, "there's no way this door was here before."

"It wasn't," Tommy replied grimly. "At least, not in our world." Rae pressed her palm against the wall, and to everyone's surprise, it rippled like a small wave and gave way with a low hiss—**a hidden door** sliding open like the entrance to some long-forgotten bunker.

Beyond the door lay a narrow flight of concrete steps, spiraling downward into pitch-black darkness. A cool breeze drifted up from below, carrying with it a strange smell—like rusted metal, old electricity, and something faintly sweet, like decayed flowers.

"Yeah, no thanks," Jinx said, backing away. "I've seen enough horror movies to know where this is going." Rae ignored him, flicking on her flashlight. "You scared?"

"Uh, yeah! Actually, I'm freakin' terrified. And you should be too!" Tommy gave Jinx a small grin. "We came this far, man. What's a few creepy steps?" Jinx groaned, throwing up his hands. "Fine. But if something jumps out, I'm shoving you down first."

The gang descended the stairs slowly, their flashlights cutting weak beams through the thick dark. The walls were cold, lined with exposed wires and cracked concrete. As they descended further, the air grew heavier, humming with an undercurrent of static—**the same static** they'd heard inside **Neon Abyss**. "Why does it feel like we're walking into the game?" Tony whispered.

"Because maybe we are," Tommy muttered. At the bottom of the stairs, they stepped into a wide underground tunnel. The walls were covered in strange symbols—**the same jagged symbols** they'd seen flash across the game screen earlier. The floor beneath their feet hummed, and old, rusted pipes ran along the ceiling, dripping with condensation.

"This place gives me the creeps," Jinx whispered, his voice echoing in the vast, empty space. Suddenly, a flicker of neon light caught Tommy's eye. At the far end of the tunnel, **a broken arcade machine** lay on its side, wires spilling from its cracked casing like entrails. The screen flickered weakly, displaying a glitched version of the mall above them—only it was twisted, corrupted, just like inside the game. "Guys," Rae whispered. "I think we're standing in what's left of the original **Neon Abyss.**"

As the gang approached the broken machine, Tommy's heart raced. He could feel it—like a strange connection thrumming between the arcade cabinet and the walls around them. Rae knelt beside the machine and traced her fingers over a metal plate bolted to its side. "Look at this." They all leaned in close. The plate was old, tarnished with rust, but they could still make out the words engraved into it: **PROPERTY OF ECLIPSE ELECTRONICS, 1979.** "Eclipse Electronics?" Jinx frowned. "Never heard of 'em."

"That's because they went out of business in 81," Tony said, adjusting his camcorder. "I read about it once. Something about... an experimental game project gone wrong."

"This must be one of their machines," Rae said, her voice tight with realization. "And somehow, it ended up here—buried under the mall."

"That's great and all," Jinx grumbled, "but why is it still *alive*?" As if in response, the machine emitted a low hum, and the flickering screen began to display **more symbols**—symbols that matched the ones on the walls. A chill ran through Tommy's spine as the realization hit him. "This isn't just a game," he whispered. "It's... **a gateway.**"

Suddenly, the machine whirred to life, and a voice—glitchy and robotic—echoed through the tunnel:

"Level One: Begin the Loop. Level Two: Face the Past. Final Level: Complete the Circle."

"It's giving us the rules," Rae said, her eyes wide. "We're still inside the game." Tommy's hands clenched into fists. "Then if we want to end this, we have to finish it—once and for all."

The screen glitched again, and **an exit door** flickered into view at the far end of the tunnel. "That's gotta be the way out," Tony said, raising his camcorder. "But something tells me it won't be that easy."

The gang sprinted toward the flickering exit, their footsteps echoing in the cold, metallic space. The walls around them buzzed with increasing intensity, and the shadows seemed to move, stretching and reaching toward them.

"Run!" Tommy shouted, gripping Jinx's arm and pulling him forward as the static buzzed louder, threatening to swallow them whole. The neon signs overhead began to twist, displaying terrifying messages: **NO ESCAPE. GAME OVER. LOST FOREVER.** But Tommy refused to give in. "Keep going!" he shouted over the roar of static.

They reached the flickering door just as the tunnel began to collapse behind them. With one final burst of speed, they threw themselves through the glowing exit—plunging into blinding white light.

When the light faded, the gang found themselves lying on the floor of **The Pixel Palace**, gasping for breath. The shattered **Neon Abyss** cabinet was gone—replaced by **an empty space**, as if it had never existed.

Tony blinked and adjusted his camcorder. "Did... did we do it? Are we out?" Jinx groaned, rubbing his head. "If we're not, I'm suing someone."

Rae sat up slowly, scanning the arcade. "I think... I think we broke the loop." Tommy let out a shaky breath, but deep down, a nagging feeling tugged at him. The **Neon Abyss** may have been destroyed, but its presence still lingered—like a song stuck on the edge of memory. The game was over... but **the Abyss** was still out there. Waiting.

Chapter 8: The Shadows of the Final Level

Tommy sat cross-legged on the sticky linoleum floor of **The Pixel Palace**, the hum of spent adrenaline still buzzing in his veins. Around him, the arcade lay in eerie silence, as if holding its breath. The empty space where **Neon Abyss** had once stood felt like a gaping wound—raw, unfinished, waiting for something to bleed back into it.

Rae paced in tight circles, her flashlight flickering in and out. "I don't get it. We finished the loop. The game's gone. So why do I feel like we're not out of the woods yet?" Jinx leaned against a pinball machine, chewing nervously on a piece of gum. "Maybe it's just PTSD," he muttered, though the joke fell flat. "We nearly got eaten by a video game. Can't exactly walk that off."

Tommy stayed quiet, but the nagging sense of **something unfinished** gnawed at him. It wasn't just the absence of the game—it was the feeling that **they had left someone behind**. "Danny," Tommy whispered. Tony lowered his camcorder, the red recording light casting an eerie glow across his face. "What do you mean?" Tommy swallowed hard. "We didn't find him. He's still... somewhere in there. The game might be gone, but the **Abyss** isn't."

The air in the arcade grew colder, and the hum of fluorescent lights flickered unevenly above them. Then, without warning, the **security monitors** mounted on the walls crackled to life—blasting static across the arcade. Tony swung his camcorder toward the noise, his pulse quickening. "What the hell?" The static shifted, glitching in and out, until a blurry **figure** appeared on the screen. It was grainy, hard to make out—but it was a kid. **Danny Fletcher.**

"Holy crap," Jinx whispered. "It's him." Danny's image flickered, his face pale and warped, like a photograph burned at the edges. His lips moved soundlessly, mouthing the same message over and over. Rae leaned closer to the screen, her heart pounding. "He's saying... 'Come find me.'" The static roared louder, and then the screen **snapped off**—leaving them in stunned silence.

"We didn't finish the game," Tommy muttered, the realization hitting him like a punch to the gut. "Not really." Rae tightened her grip on the flashlight. "Then we go back. We finish it. For Danny." The group retraced their steps through the mall, sneakers squeaking on the scuffed tile floors. The mall's eerie quiet felt heavier now, like the air had thickened with every step they took toward the arcade's hidden door.

When they reached the dark corner where the **Neon Abyss** cabinet had stood, the wall shimmered once more—just like before. The **hidden door** creaked open, revealing the narrow staircase spiraling into the darkness below.

Tommy took a deep breath. "This is it. We go down, find Danny, and end this for good." Jinx groaned, but there was no hesitation in his step. "I swear, if this turns into some *Poltergeist* crap..." Tony adjusted the camcorder on his shoulder. "Let's just make it out in one piece, alright?" With that, the gang descended into the dark once again.

The stairs felt steeper this time, the air thicker, humming with **more static** than before. As they reached the bottom, the broken machine that had once displayed **the glitched version of the mall** now flickered with **a new message:**

"FINAL LEVEL: THE TRAPPED." The walls around them seemed to pulse in sync with the flickering screen, and the symbols etched into the walls glowed faintly, their jagged lines shifting like living circuits. "This is it," Tommy whispered, heart pounding. "Danny's in there."

Rae adjusted her flashlight and stepped forward, unwavering. "Then let's go get him." The flickering screen glowed brighter, and the **doorway to the final level** opened before them—a jagged portal of neon static, crackling like broken glass. One by one, they stepped through the threshold, vanishing into the game's final gauntlet.

The gang emerged on the other side, standing in **the heart of the Abyss**—a surreal, twisted version of the **mall**, suspended in glitching time. The escalators spiraled into infinity, store windows bled neon light, and the walls stretched in impossible ways, folding into loops that seemed to swallow themselves whole.

But the mall wasn't empty. **Shadowy figures** roamed the corridors—kids trapped inside the game, their bodies warped and glitched, as if they had been here for years. "Look!" Tommy shouted, pointing down a broken hallway. There, at the edge of the glitching world, stood **Danny Fletcher**—his face pale, his eyes hollow, glowing faintly with the same blue static that had consumed Jinx in the earlier levels.

Tommy sprinted toward him, ignoring the shadows closing in around them. "Danny! We're here to get you out!" Danny's head tilted slightly, as if he barely recognized them. "You... shouldn't have come," he whispered. His voice was fractured, split across layers of static. "The game... it doesn't let anyone leave."

"We're not leaving without you," Tommy said firmly, grabbing Danny's hand. His grip was cold, like touching the surface of a broken TV screen. Rae and Tony reached them just as the walls began to **collapse**, folding inward like crumpled paper. "We need to go—now!" Rae shouted, pulling Tommy back toward the flickering exit.

But just as they turned, the **Neon Abyss itself** roared to life—its shadows twisting and converging into a massive, glitching figure. It loomed over them, its body made from shards of broken memories, missing kids body parts and neon static. **The game had become a monster.**

The gang sprinted toward the flickering exit, the shadow-monster hot on their heels. It roared, its voice a warped symphony of fear, anger, and desperation—**a thousand lost players** screaming through the static.

Tommy gripped Danny's hand tighter, refusing to let go. "Don't stop! We're almost there!" The walls folded in faster, and the ground beneath them trembled, cracking apart into pieces of glitching neon light. The exit was just ahead—a jagged portal framed in flickering static. They had seconds—maybe less. "Go! Go! Go!" Rae screamed, shoving Tony forward.

With one final burst of speed, they **threw themselves through the portal**—just as the monster reached for them, its glitching claws inches from their backs. The world imploded behind them in a deafening roar of static and shattered neon.

The gang landed hard on the floor of **The Pixel Palace**, gasping for breath. The arcade was quiet, eerily still—except for the faint hum of machines powering on around them.

Tommy looked around frantically, his heart hammering in his chest. "Danny? Danny!" There, lying beside him, was **Danny Fletcher**—whole, alive, but dazed, as if waking from a long, strange dream.

"You... you found me," Danny whispered, blinking up at them in disbelief. Tommy grinned, relief washing over him like a tidal wave. "Yeah, man. We found you."

As the gang helped Danny to his feet, the familiar hum of the arcade returned, and the lights flickered back to life. The **Neon Abyss** machine was gone—erased from existence, as if it had never been there.

For a moment, everything felt normal again. Safe.

But as they turned to leave, **a faint flicker** caught Tommy's eye—just for a second. The outline of a cabinet, hidden in the corner, buzzing softly with static.

It wasn't over. Not really.

Because some games... **never end**.

Chapter 9: Breaking the Game

The buzz of **The Pixel Palace** arcade faded behind them as the gang left the mall, their nerves still raw from the narrow escape. **Danny Fletcher** shuffled along beside them, pale and quiet, his eyes glassy, as if part of him was still trapped inside **Neon Abyss**.

The night air was cool, a welcome relief after the suffocating hum of static. **Tommy** glanced back at the darkened mall, half-expecting the flickering outline of the **arcade machine** to reappear, but the parking lot was still—too still. Rae crossed her arms. "Okay, we got Danny out, but something tells me this isn't over." She chewed her lip, her gaze flickering toward Tommy. "We need to make sure this thing is really dead. No more 'almost.'"

Danny whispered, his voice barely audible. "It's... still in there." Jinx groaned, throwing his head back. "You've gotta be kidding me. I thought the whole *running for our lives through a nightmare video game* thing was enough. What else do we have to do?"

Tommy tightened his grip on his bike handles. "We have to go back." Jinx's mouth dropped open. "We just got out!" - "This time," Tommy said, meeting Rae's determined gaze, "we don't just survive the game. **We destroy it.**"

Back in **Tony's basement**, the gang huddled together on the worn carpet, surrounded by comic books, empty soda cans, and the hum of old electronics. Danny sat silently on the couch, hugging his knees to his chest, his wide eyes still locked on the camcorder's glowing red light as if it were the only thing tethering him to reality.

Tony rewound the footage from their last trip into the arcade, pausing on a glitchy frame where the **Neon Abyss symbols** briefly appeared—those jagged, circuit-like runes that seemed more ancient than digital. "There," he said, pointing. "That's the key. These symbols... they're not just part of the game—they **are** the game."

Rae leaned in closer, tracing the glowing runes with her finger on the TV screen. "So, if we can destroy these symbols, we destroy the game." Jinx raised an eyebrow. "You know how to destroy ancient, cursed game runes, genius?" Rae smirked. "Not yet. But I have a plan."

The next morning, the gang gathered in front of a dimly lit storefront across from the mall: **Madame Seraphina's Fortune & Flame,** a small occult shop filled with crystals, incense, and strange artifacts. The bell above the door jingled as they entered, and the air was thick with the scent of sage and cinnamon.

Madame Seraphina, draped in flowing robes, looked up from behind the counter with an amused smile. "Well, if it isn't my favorite group of adventurers. Let me guess—you're not here for tarot readings."

Tommy stepped forward. "We need your help. There's... a game, and it's not just a game. We have to destroy it." Madame Seraphina's smile faded. "Ah. **The Abyss.**" She spoke the name as if it weighed heavily on her tongue. "I knew it would resurface eventually."

"You know about it?" Rae asked, surprised.

Madame Seraphina nodded solemnly. "It's older than it appears—an ancient doorway disguised in modern skin. A game that feeds on fear and never truly ends." She reached beneath the counter and produced **a black, leather-bound book**, its pages worn and yellowed with age. "If you want to destroy it, you'll need to perform **a ritual of severance**—one that binds the symbols and burns them from reality."

She opened the book to a page filled with strange glyphs—**the same symbols** they had seen inside the game. "You'll need these," she said, handing them a small pouch filled with **black salt**, seven **candles**, and a **silver dagger** inscribed with protective runes. "And one last thing—the ritual can only be completed by those who have touched the Abyss." Tommy glanced at his friends. "That's us."

The gang returned to the mall that evening, carrying Madame Seraphina's supplies in their backpacks. The sky was a bruised shade of purple, and the air buzzed with quiet anticipation, as if the whole world was holding its breath. The arcade was waiting.

They stepped inside and were greeted by **the faint hum of static**—a sound that seemed to pulse from the very walls, as if the arcade itself was alive. **The hidden door** behind the **Neon Abyss** machine shimmered once more, inviting them back into the darkness below.

"This is it," Tommy said, gripping the pouch of black salt. "We go down, we perform the ritual, and we end this." - "Yeah," Jinx muttered, shifting nervously. "Or it ends us."

They descended the narrow staircase one last time, the air growing colder and thicker with each step. The walls seemed to pulse with static, and the neon symbols glowed brighter as they reached the bottom—where the **broken arcade machine** still flickered weakly in the center of the room. "Alright," Rae said, pulling out the black salt. "Let's get to work."

They formed a **circle** around the machine, placing the seven candles at even intervals along the edge. North, South, East, West, Above, Below, Within. Tony lit each one, the flames flickering wildly as if caught in a wind that didn't exist. The air buzzed with tension, and the shadows along the walls **twitched and shifted**, like something waiting to strike.

Rae scattered the black salt and grave dirt gathered under a waning moonlit night in a wide circle, muttering under her breath. "This better work." Tommy pulled out the silver dagger, the protective runes gleaming in the candlelight. "What do I do with this?"

"Draw the symbols," Rae instructed. "We need to recreate them—then destroy them." As Tommy began carving the symbols into the dirt with the dagger, the arcade machine roared to life. **The static grew louder**, the glitching screen flashing violently as **shadowy figures** emerged from the walls—warped, twisted versions of the people the game had claimed.

"It's trying to stop us!" Jinx yelled, backing away from one of the figures, some type of shadowing T.V. static thing, as it lunged toward him. "Keep going!" Rae shouted, kicking over one of the shadows. "We're almost there!"

Tommy's hand trembled, but he kept carving, the silver dagger glinting with each stroke. The symbols glowed brighter as he etched them into the earth, and the air around them pulsed, heavy with electricity.

The shadows swirled closer, but Tony stepped forward, holding his camcorder like a shield. "Smile, you glitchy bastards," he muttered, the red recording light blinking defiantly.

The final symbol was drawn, and the ground beneath them **rumbled** violently. The arcade machine screeched, the screen warping as if it were imploding on itself. "Now!" Rae shouted. "Say the spell!" The gang recited the incantation Madame Seraphina had given them, their voices steady despite the chaos around them:

"By the seven flames that bind this space,

By the salt that circles and seals,

Return now to your shadowed place—

No more to walk, no more to steal."

The candles flared brightly, and the shadows recoiled, shrieking as the salt circle blazed with a sudden light like gunpowder lit from a fuse. The arcade machine let out one final, desperate **scream**—then exploded into **a burst of static and sparks**, collapsing into nothingness. The room fell silent. The game was gone.

The gang stood in stunned silence, panting and clutching each other, the candles still flickering softly in the darkness. Jinx let out a breathless laugh. "We did it... We actually did it."

Rae grinned, wiping sweat from her brow. "Yeah. And I don't ever want to see another arcade machine again." Tommy stared at the spot where the **Neon Abyss** had once stood, a strange sense of peace washing over him. The game was finished. **The loop was broken.**

They had won. As they made their way back up the stairs, the static hum of the Abyss finally faded into silence—leaving nothing behind but **the soft glow of victory.**

Chapter 10: Glitched Reality

Asoft breeze blew through the empty parking lot of **Sunset Hills Mall**, stirring paper cups and discarded receipts along the cracked pavement. The gang leaned against their BMX bikes, bathed in the dim orange glow of flickering streetlights. The night felt lighter—like a storm that had passed, leaving only the cool stillness behind.

"We did it," Rae whispered, brushing a lock of hair out of her eyes. Her flashlight dangled loosely from her hand, flickering slightly. "The game's gone. For real this time." Jinx leaned on his bike handlebars, still catching his breath. "No more portals. No more glitchy monsters. No more *Neon Abyss*." He grinned wide. "Feels good, right?"

Tommy nodded, but deep down, something gnawed at him—like a splinter in his mind that he couldn't quite pull free. He glanced back at the mall, the silent windows reflecting the night sky. It felt... too quiet. "Yeah," Tommy murmured. "We're finally out." But part of him wasn't so sure.

The next morning, Tommy woke to the sound of birds chirping outside his window. The sun streamed through the curtains, and for the first time in days, the air felt normal. **Danny Fletcher** was safe. The game was gone. And life was supposed to go back to the way it had been before. But it didn't. Not really.

Tommy sat at the breakfast table, absentmindedly poking at his cereal as the hum of the refrigerator filled the silence. Across the table, Danny ate quietly, still a little pale but slowly coming back to himself.

Tommy's mom leaned against the counter, flipping through the newspaper. "It's nice to see you boys getting outside again," she said with a warm smile. "All that time at the arcade... It was starting to get unhealthy." Danny gave a weak smile but didn't say anything.

Tommy stirred his cereal, the spoon clinking against the bowl. He couldn't shake the nagging thought that had been following him since last night: *What if the game isn't really gone?*

Later that afternoon, Tommy met up with Rae, Jinx, and Tony in the **backyard of Sandy's house**—their usual hangout. They sat cross-legged on the grass, swapping jokes and stories, trying to pretend things were normal.

Tony played back the footage on his camcorder, grinning as the screen displayed their final moments in the **Abyss**. "Man, this is gonna make one hell of a story."

Jinx snorted. "No one's gonna believe us." Rae chuckled, but her gaze drifted toward the **mall** in the distance. The big giant C looming over the entrance towards the arcade and food court. "Even if they did... Some things are better left alone."

Tommy nodded. But just as he looked away, something strange caught his eye—a reflection in the **glass door** of Sandy's porch. For a brief second, he saw it: **the faint, flickering outline of the Neon Abyss cabinet.** It blinked in and out like a faulty bulb, and then... it was gone.

Tommy's heart skipped a beat. He blinked, rubbing his eyes, but the reflection had vanished. "Did you see that?" Tommy whispered, nudging Rae. "See what?" she asked, raising an eyebrow. Tommy shook his head. "Nothing. It's... nothing."

That night, as Tommy lay in bed, sleep came slowly. He tossed and turned, the events of the past week playing on a loop in his mind. **The game**, the **maze**, the **shadow-monsters**—it all felt distant now, like the memory of a bad dream that was starting to fade.

But just as Tommy drifted off, he heard it: the soft *clink* of a coin falling onto the floor. His eyes snapped open, heart pounding. He sat up slowly, his room bathed in shadows. For a moment, everything was still. Then he spotted something glimmering in the dim light—a **token** lying on the carpet by his bed.

It wasn't just any token. It was from **The Pixel Palace**. And stamped across its surface were the words: **"One more game."** Tommy's breath hitched, his pulse racing as he stared at the coin. He wasn't out. None of them were.

The next morning, Tommy met Rae and the others outside the **mall**, clutching the token in his fist. The sky overhead was dull and gray, clouds swirling like static on a screen.

"I found this," Tommy whispered, holding out the token. Rae's eyes widened. "How... How is that possible?" Jinx paled. "No. Nope. No way. I am *not* going back in there." Tony adjusted his camcorder, a grim expression on his face. "We don't have a choice. If the game's still running, it means the door isn't closed."

Tommy nodded. "One more game. That's what it said." They all exchanged uneasy glances, the weight of the truth settling over them like a heavy blanket. The game wasn't over. It was just... **waiting.**

With a sense of grim determination, the gang made their way toward **Sunset Hills Mall** for what they knew would be their last mission. The arcade loomed ahead, its neon sign flickering weakly, as if it, too, was caught in a loop.

Tommy glanced at his friends—Rae, Jinx, Tony, and Danny—and gave a small, determined nod. "This time, we finish it for good." Jinx exhaled sharply, gripping his skateboard like a lifeline. "If I get sucked into another dimension, I'm haunting you all." Rae smirked. "You already haunt us. What's one more ghost?"

They all laughed, the sound light but tinged with fear. Then, without another word, they pushed through the glass doors and stepped into **The Pixel Palace**—ready to face whatever came next. The arcade machine buzzed softly, the familiar hum of **Neon Abyss** returning as if it had never left. The screen blinked to life, swirling with jagged lines and glitching symbols.

Tommy slipped the token into the machine. It landed with a soft *clink,* and the game whirred to life, the words flashing across the screen:

"FINAL ROUND: PLAY TO WIN." Tommy gripped the joystick, his heart steady. This time, he knew what to expect. The game might be a trap, a nightmare disguised in neon—but it wasn't unbeatable. Not anymore. He looked back at his friends, their faces set with determination. They had survived the Abyss before. Now, they were going to **beat it.** The screen flickered, and the robotic voice echoed through the arcade:

"Level One: Begin."

Tommy smiled. "Let's do this."

The game started.

Also by B. Humphrey

Retro Horrors: The Lost Decade
The Arcade Incident

The Autumn Folklore Chronicles
The Forest Of Forgotten Names
The Witch Of Windspindle Hollow
The Burrowfolk Chronicles

The Phantom Finders Club
A Haunting On Maplewood Street
The Secrets Of Old Fort Tower
Ghosts OF The Infirmary

www.ingramcontent.com/pod-product-compliance
Lightning Source LLC
Chambersburg PA
CBHW070823170726
48000CB00019B/2451